Justice For Cassidy

Written and Illustrated By
Andre Sullivan

Andre Sullivan/Hamilton Jackson Publishing LLC

605 Sumter Street

Greenville, SC 29617

www.andresullivan.com

Publishers Note: This is a work of fiction. Names, characters, places, or incidents are a product of the authors imagination. Locales and public names are sometimes used for atmospheric purposes. Any resemblance to actual people, living or dead, or to businesses, companies, events, institutions, or locales is completely coincidental.

Cover Design by: Jamaal Williams

For ordering information, please contact the author at the address above.

Greenville/Andre Sullivan-First Edition

ISBN- 978-0-9968489-5-4

"Dedicated to unarmed historically disenfranchised gunned down by police brutality."

"Injustice anywhere is a threat to justice everywhere."
-Dr. King

Right and wrong
Is not always easy
It takes time and love
To find the real meaning.

"Right and wrong
That's totally easy!"
Cassidy exclaimed
While watching some TV.

"Bad guys look bad
They do bad things.
What's hard about that?
What else could he mean?"

Cassidy walked to the room
Where her parents were reading.
She began to tell them
What she saw on TV.

A story about a woman named Justice
And how she couldn't see.
"Is that why she can't tell bad guys
From you or me?"

Think to yourself ;
What if people were books?
You wouldn't want someone to judge you
based on how you look.

You'd want them to read you
page after page.
Growing to understand you
in brand new ways.

True justice is everyone
having a fair chance.
Not being judged by looks,
or first glance.

"Oh no!
What ever will I do?"
Screamed Ms. W
From tall house 22.

The family sprang from the house
and what did they see?
Ms. W. was crying.
Something was missing.

"What's wrong Ms. W?"
Cassidy's mom sat beside her.
"My favorite toucan is missing!
Come back to me MYRA!"

"Things have gone missing,
more often than not.
Looks like we have
sticky fingers on our block."

At that very moment
the infamous Jean Jenkins was walking
down the street.
With a toucan in hand,
"A thief! A thief!"

Jean looked left then right
"You talking to me?
I didn't steal Myra,
I got Eugene this week."

Cassidy's father laughed
"Well that settles that."
But Ms. W was not pleased.
Not pleased indeed.

"This is not over!
I'll prove it was you.
You're a bad kid Jean,
I've got my eye on you."

Did Jean take the bird?
Cassidy wouldn't take a stance.
He was sort of a bully,
but he still deserved a chance.

"I'll find Myra, Ms. W,
leave it all to me.
I'll bring her back and serve some justice
just you wait and see."

Day after day
She looked high and looked low
Connecting the dots
But she still didn't know.

One neighbor after the other
she gathered information .
A bird , a ball
A frisbee , and fake bacon .

Jean had all three of these
and they were pretty new .
This didn't look good for Jean
from tall house 32 .

There was only one person
that remained on her list.
The infamous Jean Jenkins!
She felt this was it.

All the facts and clues
pointed straight to Jean.
The bird, the ball,
the bacon, and frisbee.

She charged down the block
"I know it was you!"
While she raced to confront Jean
from tall house 32.

She got to Jean's house,
and couldn't believe what she'd seen.
Jean was a scout.
He was helping older ladies cross the street.

Saying please and thank you
with a great big grin.
This was not the Jean she knew.
Could he be a clone? A twin?

Think to yourself;
What if people were books?
You wouldn't want someone to judge you
based on how you look.

You'd want them to read you,
page after page.
Growing to understand you
in brand new ways.

At that moment
She made a decision.
To prove Jean was innocent,
and find what's gone missing.

She asks for Jeans help
To solve the case.
But Ms. W. was not pleased.
Not please indeed.

She knew it was Jean
regardless of facts.
Jean was bad kid
anyone could see that.

Determined as ever ,
the two teamed up .
Combing the neighborhood
for everyone's stuff .

They found the fake bacon
buried near a tree .
They also found the frisbee
with bite marks from teeth .

They found the lost ball
slobbered and chewed .
The 2 smiled with Joy
They finally had a clue .

Cassidy and Jean
traveled door to door
returning what was lost.
They even got rewards.

But, Cassidy felt bad.
She made a promise she didn't keep.
They didn't find Myra,
and Ms. W was going to freak.

With their heads hung low
they approached the door.
Just before they knocked
they heard a sound to explore.

They went around the back,
and what did they see?
Winston the dog and Myra
sharing tea.

Just then
Winston walked over.
with Myra in his mouth
Ms. W. fell over.

Myra was ruined
from being buried and chewed.
Jean looked to Cassidy.
He knew what he had to do.

Jean went to Ms. W.
"I'm sorry that happened to you.
Please take my bird.
You can call him Myra 2."

Ms. W. smiled
taking Winston and Jean in her arms.
You be sure to visit.
You can see Myra whenever you want.

True justice is everyone
having a fair chance.
Not being judged by looks,
or first glance.

Titles also available by Andre Sullivan

Just Like Me

Cassidy Puts On A Show

For more information please visit
www.AndreSullivan.com

Made in the USA
Columbia, SC
16 July 2020